For "Smilin' Jim," my inspiration, my father

SIMON & SCHUSTER BOOKS FOR YOUNG READERS

An imprint of Simon & Schuster Children's Publishing Division

1230 Avenue of the Americas, New York, New York 10020

Copyright © 2014 by Ronald Barrett

All rights reserved, including the right of reproduction in whole or in part in any form.

SIMON & SCHUSTER BOOKS FOR YOUNG READERS is a trademark of Simon & Schuster, Inc.

For information about special discounts for bulk purchases, please contact Simon & Schuster

Special Sales at 1-866-506-1949 or business@simonandschuster.com.

The Simon & Schuster Speakers Bureau can bring authors to your live event. For more information

or to book an event, contact the Simon & Schuster Speakers Bureau at 1-866-248-3049 or

visit our website at www.simonspeakers.com.

Book design by Ron Barrett

The text for this book is set in Gill Sans Std.

The illustrations for this book are rendered in pencil, watercolor, and ink.

Manufactured in China

0714 SCP

2 4 6 8 10 9 7 5 3 1

Library of Congress Cataloging-in-Publication Data

Barrett, Ron, author, illustrator.

Cats got talent / Ronald Barrett.—First edition.

pages cm

"A Paula Wiseman book."

Summary: When three cats find themselves homeless in an alley, they form a singing group with the hope that

they will earn the love they need.

ISBN 978-1-4424-9451-0 (hardcover : alk. paper)

ISBN 978-1-4424-9452-7 (eBook)

[1. Cats—Fiction.] I. Title.

PZ7.B275346Cat 2014

[E]—dc23

2013012400

CATS GOT TALENT

Written and Illustrated by Ron Barrett

A Paula Wiseman Book

Simon & Schuster Books for Young Readers

New York   London   Toronto   Sydney   New Delhi

There were three cats
who lived in an alley.

There was Hal, who only had one thought.

Hal was once a pet to a family.

But he had some despicable habits.

So they felt he had to be gotten rid of.

Dora once lived in a dress store.

She longed to wear the
beautiful clothing she saw
the women wear.

Unfortunately, she also liked to pretend she was the clothing,

and the customers got frightened.

So the owner had to ask her to leave.

Geneva was formerly a pet to a star.

**But the star made some movies that nobody liked,
and her career took a turn for the worse.**

So she could no longer afford a chef, a butler, a maid, a gardener, or a cat.

**And that's how Hal, Dora, and Geneva came to the alley,
where they met one night over dinner.**

They discovered that they enjoyed singing and doing things together.

One day Hal read that singers earned big money.

"If I had big money," said Hal,
"I'd never be hungry. I could really stuff myself."

"Mmmmm yeah," said Dora. "I could get some high heels,
a hat, and maybe some jewels to go with them."

"And I could really be taken care of," said Geneva.

So they began to practice where they thought no one could hear them.

At least they *thought* no one could hear them.

After several weeks of rehearsing, they thought they were good enough to have their opening night in the alley.

The audience was settled in their beds.

The curtain opened.

The light went on.

And the cats began to sing.

At first the audience was hushed.

They listened very intently.

"Food!" cried Hal.
"Clothes!" said Dora. "Beautiful hats and shoes!"
"Gifts!" said Geneva. "Love. They really love us."

The cats had gotten all they wanted, so they stopped singing.
And their audience was very happy indeed.

But some cats can never have enough.